FOURTH GRAD
SUPER SALESMAN
ROCK STAR

Danny Dorfman rings the doorbell. A beautiful girl answers the door. Her incredible blue eyes just stare at him with awe.

"Mother," she calls, "you will never guess who is here. It is Danny Dorfman!"

"The world's greatest salesman?" asks the mother, running into the room.

"Yes, at our very own house!"

"Please," the mother begs Danny, "tell us what we can buy."

"How about some candy bars?" he says.

"We will take ten thousand," says the mother.

The girl doesn't say anything. She just keeps staring at Danny.

"I also play the guitar," says Danny.

Danny Dorfman's Dream Band #2

MEET MAXIMUM CLYDE

RONALD KIDD

Illustrated by Bob Jones

Puffin Books

PUFFIN BOOKS
Published by the Penguin Group
Penguin Books USA Inc.,
375 Hudson Street, New York, New York 10014, U.S.A.
Penguin Books Ltd, 27 Wrights Lane, London W8 5TZ, England
Penguin Books Australia Ltd, Ringwood, Victoria, Australia
Penguin Books Canada Ltd, 10 Alcorn Avenue, Toronto, Ontario, Canada M4V 3B2
Penguin Books (N.Z.) Ltd, 182–190 Wairau Road, Auckland 10, New Zealand

Penguin Books Ltd, Registered Offices: Harmondsworth, Middlesex, England

First published in the United States of America by Puffin Books,
a division of Penguin Books USA Inc., 1992

1 3 5 7 9 10 8 6 4 2

Library of Congress Catalog Card Number: 92-60107
ISBN: 0-14-034989-8

Printed in the United States of America
Set in Century Schoolbook

To my prizewinning niece,
Lilli Loscutoff

MEET MAXIMUM CLYDE

Chapter One

The great Danny Dorfman Band was getting ready to practice.

There was Anna Lopez. She liked to hit things. Luckily, she played the drums.

There was J. Rodney Jones. Rodney played the bass. He was nearly tall enough to reach all the notes.

There was Winifred Dorfman, one of

Danny's younger sisters. She played a piano thing. It was like a row of piano keys that you plugged into the wall. The only reason Winifred was in the band was because Danny's mother had said so.

Not many people knew about the great Danny Dorfman Band, because the band had played only one concert so far. That had been at the school talent contest. The band had received an award for most exciting performance. No one in the audience would ever forget the excitement of Danny's nose accidentally hitting the stage and bleeding during the performance of his smash hit, "Too Bad, Baby."

Today the band was in the Dorfmans' garage, setting up for a rehearsal.

Everyone was there except for one person.

"Where is Danny?" asked Anna.

Just then the door opened, and Danny Dorfman came running in. He was carrying his schoolbooks. He had a big smile on his face.

"Oh boy," Danny said, hopping up and down. "Oh boy, oh boy, oh boy."

"Yo, Dorfman," said Rodney. "Try to relax."

"I can't," said Danny. "I was talking to Mrs. Parker after school, and she told me the most incredible thing."

"You passed your spelling test?" said his sister.

"More incredible than that."

"School is closed for the rest of the year?" said Anna.

"Much more incredible than that."

"Yo," said Rodney, "Martians landed on the playground?"

Danny shook his head. Every time he bounced, his voice bounced. "There's going to be a contest to raise money for the school. All of us will sell candy bars. Whoever sells the most wins a prize."

"Big deal," said Winifred. "We do that every year."

"This year it *is* a big deal," said Danny. "Ask me what the prize is."

"What's the prize?" asked Anna.

Danny's bouncing face glowed like a huge spotlight. "Four tickets to the sold-out Maximum Clyde concert."

Maximum Clyde finishes the concert with an awesome guitar solo. Then he goes to the microphone.

"Most people say I am the greatest guitar player who ever lived. But someone even greater is in the audience tonight. His name is Danny Dorfman."

The crowd goes wild as rock superstar Danny Dorfman comes forward. They reach out to touch him, just so they can find out what someone so wonderful feels like.

When Danny gets up on stage, Maximum Clyde shakes his hand and begs Danny to play. The world's two most famous guitar players turn to the audience and perform Danny's well-known hit, "Too Bad, Baby."

"Yo," Rodney asked Danny's sister, "is he okay?"

"It's just another one of his stupid daydreams," said Winifred. She walked up to Danny and yelled, "Cut it out."

Danny stared past her with a funny little smile on his face. He waved to the cheering crowd. "Hey, I love you guys."

"I hope he's not talking to me," said Anna.

Winifred clapped her hands in front of Danny's face with a sharp *crack*. His eyebrows shot up, and he made one last, very high bounce. When he came back to earth he looked around.

"Oh, hello," he said.

"You are something else," said Rodney.

"We need to win those tickets," Danny said. "And I have a plan."

Winifred closed her eyes. "Uh-oh."

"What's wrong?" asked Anna.

"Danny always has a plan. His last plan was to paint numbers on dogs so if they got lost they could be identified by police helicopters."

"Cool," said Rodney.

"Anyway," Danny told them, "this is my plan. All of us enter the contest. We go out there and sell lots of candy bars. And here is the good part. We promise that whoever wins will use the four tickets to take the rest of the band to see Maximum Clyde."

"What's so great about that?" asked Winifred.

"Don't you see?" said Danny. "We will have four chances to win instead of just one."

"What if we still don't win?" asked Anna.

Danny could hardly believe his ears. "Of course we will win. We are the great Danny Dorfman Band."

Chapter Two

The first day of the contest, the band met at Danny Dorfman's house after school. Danny handed out sheets of paper.

"What are these?" Anna asked.

"The Danny Dorfman Band pledge," he said. "Please read along with me."

I pledge, they read, *to be a good member of the Danny Dorfman Band, which means I will sell thousands of candy bars to people of all ages. Then I will share whatever Maximum Clyde tickets I get with anyone in the band who might be interested in going.*

"But I can't sell thousands of candy bars," said Winifred.

"You should have thought of that before you took the pledge," said Danny.

They went out into the front yard. Danny told them what a historic moment this was. Then he sent them off in four different directions to sell, sell, sell.

Anna Lopez did not even like Maximum Clyde. She thought anybody who used more mascara than her big sister had a problem. But Anna loved the Danny Dorfman Band. It was the greatest thing that had ever happened to her. She did not want to let Danny down. So she was going to sell candy bars. Lots of them.

Anna knocked on the door of her first house. She may have knocked a little too hard, because it sounded like bombs exploding. Nobody came to the door. After a long time, someone peeked out a window.

Anna shouted, "Hey, you!" She ran over to the window, but before she got there the curtain was pulled down.

Anna decided to knock a little softer at the next house. Instead of bombs exploding, it sounded more like street construction. This time the door opened just a crack. One eye peered out.

"What do you want?" asked the eye.

"I am selling candy bars," Anna said.

"I don't need any."

"Yes, you do," said Anna.

The door slammed shut.

At the next house she decided to be her very nicest self. She didn't even knock. She rang the doorbell. A small, thin boy opened the door.

"Hello," he said.

It was going perfectly.

"Would you like to buy some candy bars?" Anna asked him.

"Is this for charity?" he asked.

"It is for Saddler Street School."

He got this amazed look on his face. "You are in elementary school? Boy, are you huge!"

About three seconds later you couldn't see his amazed look anymore. The only thing you could see was the top of his head. That was because Anna was sitting on him.

"I don't like it when people say I am huge," she said.

A muffled voice came from somewhere underneath Anna. "I will take three candy bars," said the voice.

Winifred Dorfman was nervous. She could not decide which house to go to first.

She could try the big house with white shutters. It probably had enough room inside for twenty or so people. But maybe those people were on a special diet of oat bran and no candy bars.

The little yellow house with daisies in the yard seemed like a friendly place. But maybe it was too friendly. Winifred hated it when people kept talking to you and wouldn't let you leave.

The house on the corner looked nice.

But there was a blue rubber bone on the front porch. The people who lived there might own a vicious, man-eating dog.

All the houses made Winifred nervous. She needed to calm down. So she sat under a tree to think.

While she was thinking, she opened up her box and looked at the candy bars. They looked nice from the outside. But how could she be sure there was chocolate inside? There was only one way to find out.

Winifred took the wrapper off one candy bar and saw something dark brown. It was the color of chocolate. But it was also the color of roast beef and shoe leather. She took a bite. It tasted like chocolate. But what about the other so-called candy bars?

The next half-hour went by quickly. When it was over, Winifred knew several things: (1) she was too full to be nervous anymore; (2) at least seven of the wrappers had chocolate inside; and (3) if she ever saw another candy bar, she was going to throw up.

It was hard to tell when J. Rodney Jones was excited. He didn't jump up and down, like Danny. He didn't hit things, like Anna. He didn't get nervous, like Winifred. He would just straighten his sunglasses and smile. That's what he was doing right now.

Rodney thought that if he could just get a good start today, he might be able to sell more candy bars than anybody else. Then he would win the contest.

That would prove he was about the coolest person in the whole school.

As he knocked on the door of his first house, he wondered how many candy bars he would sell there. Maybe one or two. Maybe seventy-nine or more.

The door opened, and Mrs. Bing looked out. Mrs. Bing was a tiny lady with gray hair who spent most of her time watching TV. "Come in," she told Rodney before he could say anything. It seemed like a good sign. Rodney followed her in.

Rodney started to tell Mrs. Bing about the candy bars. But she turned on the TV and said, "Let's watch game shows."

Rodney hated game shows, but he didn't say anything. After a few minutes Rodney tried to talk about the candy bars. "Just a minute," said Mrs. Bing. "This is the good part."

Soon a commercial started, and Rodney tried again. "Not now," Mrs. Bing said. "I love commercials."

The good parts and commercials lasted a long time. When it started getting dark outside, Rodney stood up to leave.

"I hope you had a good time," said Mrs. Bing.

Rodney did not answer. He had had a terrible time. He had wasted the whole afternoon.

When Rodney got to the door, he saw that Mrs. Bing was smiling. "Thank you for coming over," she said. "That was the nicest thing that's happened to me in weeks."

Rodney walked home. He had not sold a single candy bar. He had not even talked about candy bars. But maybe he had not wasted his time after all.

Chapter Three

Danny Dorfman rings the doorbell. A beautiful girl answers the door. Her incredible blue eyes just stare at him with awe.

"Mother," she calls, "you will never guess who is here. It is Danny Dorfman!"

"The world's greatest salesman?" asks the mother, running into the room.

"Yes, at our very own house!"

"Please," the mother begs Danny, "tell us what we can buy."

"How about some candy bars?" he says.

"We will take ten thousand," says the mother.

The girl doesn't say anything. She just keeps staring at Danny.

"I also play the guitar," says Danny.

"You also what?" asked a voice.

Danny blinked his eyes. Someone was staring at him, but it wasn't a beautiful girl. It was a man with hair sticking out of the front of his shirt.

"Well?" said the man.

"Would you like to buy a candy bar?" Danny asked. "It's to raise money for Saddler Street School."

"Sorry, kid," said the man. He shut the door. He did not seem to recognize the great Danny Dorfman.

Next door was someone who did recognize Danny. It was Sweetheart, Mrs. Potter's pet Chihuahua. Sweetheart stuck her pointy little head through a hole in the fence and started yapping as loudly as she could. Mrs. Potter came to the door before Danny even knocked.

"Sweetheart is my little watchdog," Mrs. Potter told him. "Isn't she wonderful?"

"Yes," said Danny.

"Are you selling candy bars, too?" asked Mrs. Potter.

Danny did not like the sound of that.

"Would you like to buy one?" he asked.

"You know what they say," she told

him. “The early bird gets the worm.”

Danny did not know why she was talking about worms. He wanted to talk about candy bars.

“Jimmy Karas was here first,” she said. “I bought two candy bars from him, and I’m afraid I don’t need any more.”

Danny’s face must have had a sad look on it, because Mrs. Potter patted his shoulder. “There, there,” she said, “it’s all right. To make you feel better, I’ll give you a nice surprise. You can play with Sweetheart.”

“Really, that’s not necessary,” said Danny.

Mrs. Potter felt that it was necessary. She sipped lemonade and smiled as she watched Sweetheart chase Danny around the yard.

"Why don't you scratch Sweetheart under the chin?" Mrs. Potter suggested. "She loves it when people do that."

But Danny could not scratch Sweetheart under the chin, because the chin was moving too fast. Also, there were teeth attached to it.

"Thank you for giving Sweetheart so much exercise," Mrs. Potter said when Danny left.

"You are welcome," Danny called over his shoulder as he ran off down the street. He wanted to get as far away from Sweetheart as possible. He ran for a long time, and then he turned down a new street. That was when it happened.

He heard Maximum Clyde music.

It was one of the most fabulous moments of Danny Dorfman's life. It was like a magic sign from Maximum Clyde himself. The song seemed to be saying, *Don't give up, Danny. You can do it. You can win the contest.* Actually, the name of the song was "Get Out of My Face."

Danny followed the music to a small house with weeds growing in the front yard. As he got closer the music got louder. But there was another sound coming from inside the house. It was the sound of children playing.

Danny thought about how children love candy bars. And he started to walk faster. Soon he was running. This could be the house he had been waiting for.

Chapter Four

Danny knocked on the door. While he waited, he noticed that the porch was dirty. There were empty soda cans and trash on it. There were spiderwebs. There was dust everywhere. Perhaps the house had not been visited for thousands of years.

Danny waited a long time. No one came to the door. He thought maybe it was because the music and the children were so loud. So he knocked harder. Still no one came.

What would Maximum Clyde do in this situation? Danny didn't know, because it was hard to think of Maximum Clyde selling candy bars.

There was a little window in the front door. Through the window Danny could see three children playing inside. There were twenty-four candy bars in his box. It was perfect. The children could each buy eight candy bars.

Danny tapped on the window, but the children just kept playing. They did not even look at him. Suddenly Danny knew why. They were zombies from outer space. Their ship had landed on Earth, and they had found this deserted house to live in.

* * *

A hand touches Danny's shoulder. He turns around and sees one of the zombies standing behind him. She looks like a seven-year-old girl, but her true age is six hundred ninety-two.

"My name is Zondor," she says.

"I am Danny Dorfman," he answers. "The people of Earth welcome you."

"We came to your world for Maximum Clyde music and candy bars," says Zondor. She reaches into Danny's box and takes a candy bar. Then she eats it.

"Don't you want to take off the wrapper?" asks Danny.

"That is the best part," Zondor answers.

She buys all the candy bars in Danny's box. Then she buys all the candy bars in the whole school.

"Please come back to our planet with us," Zondor begs Danny. "You can be king of all the zombies."

It is a hard choice to make, but Danny decides to stay on Earth and be a rock superstar.

He helps the zombies load the candy bars into their zombie spaceship.

"Goodbye, Danny Dorfman," says Zondor. "We will always remember you."

And that is why to this day there is a statue of Danny Dorfman on the planet of the zombies.

Danny heard a noise. He turned around. There was somebody standing there, but it was not Zondor. It was a boy who was two or three years older than Danny. He was wearing clothes

that had patches on them. He did not look very happy.

"Who are you?" asked the boy.

"Danny Dorfman."

"We don't like people snooping around our house," the boy said.

"I knocked on the door," Danny explained. "Maybe you didn't hear me."

"We heard you. Now go away and don't come back."

Danny wanted to ask the boy about the Maximum Clyde music. He wanted to sell him eight or more candy bars. But before Danny could say anything else, the boy walked into the house and shut the door behind him.

Chapter Five

Most people would have been crushed by what had happened to Danny. They would go off to a desert island and cry just about all the time. Danny did not do that. That is why he is called the great Danny Dorfman.

The very next day Danny was running around the neighborhood like a world-champion candy bar seller. He

made little signs that said CANDY BARS FOR SALE with his name and phone number. Then he drew pictures of dinosaurs on the signs, and he put them up at the grocery store and the donut shop. He went through two boxes of candy bars in two days and went back to school for more.

It was Wednesday. The contest would end Monday. Danny had sold fifty-one candy bars. He thought he was doing well, but he did not know how well. So he thought of a plan to find out how everybody else was doing. It was totally brilliant.

Danny went around telling people they had been picked for a special survey. He asked them if they could name a very delicious food that came in a wrapper and was made out of chocolate.

Then he asked them if they had ever sold this food. If so, how many?

The more people Danny talked to, the more excited he got. No one was close to his amazing total of fifty-one candy bars. He could almost hear the Maximum Clyde concert playing in his head.

Then he talked to Mimi Spinoli. Actually, Mimi Spinoli talked to him.

"We know what you are doing, Danny Dorfman," she said. Mimi was with her twin sister, Mitzi. When you looked at them, just about all you could see were freckles and red hair. Then they opened their mouths, and the flash of silver braces almost blinded you. Danny called their mouths Jaws of Death.

"What do you mean?" asked Danny.

Mitzi smiled with her Jaws of Death. "We heard about your so-called survey, which is really to find out who has sold the most candy bars."

Danny felt his face get hot. How did the Spinoli twins know his secret?

"We can save you all that work," Mimi said. "The answer to your question is me. I have sold the most candy bars."

"I suppose it is more than fifty-one, which have been sold by a mystery person who asked me not to reveal his or her name," said Danny. He probably should not have told them that number, but he wanted to see the Jaws of Death open wide in surprise.

Mimi and Mitzi looked at each other and laughed. Mimi said, "I have sold three boxes, which for your feeble brain means seventy-two candy bars."

Danny did not have Jaws of Death.

All he had were jaws of teeth. They opened wide in surprise, just the way Mimi and Mitzi's jaws were supposed to have opened.

"That is twenty-one more candy bars than your mystery person, which is you," said Mitzi. The twins laughed again. Danny thought they sounded like monkeys that you might find at the zoo.

Just then, Danny had another totally brilliant idea.

"How many candy bars have you sold?" he asked Mitzi.

She got this funny look on her face. "What do you mean?"

"You have sold zero candy bars. Isn't that right?"

"Well, yes," she said nervously. "I am not in the contest."

"Yes, you are," said Danny. "You are both calling yourself Mimi, then selling candy bars and adding them up to equal seventy-two. Which, by the way, is called cheating."

Mitzi did not say no. She did not say yes. She said, "Prove it."

The Spinoli twins looked just like each other. No one could ever prove that they were both selling candy bars.

Danny tried to think of what he could do. Maybe his band could add up their candy bars, too. But Winifred did not look very much like Rodney. And Anna was a little taller than Danny. It probably would not work. Of course, the main reason they could not do it was that the great Danny Dorfman does not cheat.

There was only one thing Danny could do.

"Maybe I will give up," he said.

Mimi and Mitzi smiled with their Jaws of Death. Maybe they would get too confident and stop selling candy bars. If they did, they would be in trouble. Because Danny was going to start selling harder than ever.

Chapter Six

For the rest of the week, Danny used all his extra time to sell candy bars. He tried everything he could think of.

He stood outside the bank, because he thought people coming out would have lots of money. He told them they should invest in candy bars.

He went to the carpet store, because it had a nice soft floor that was perfect for getting on his knees to plead.

He went to the barber shop, where people sitting in barber chairs could not walk away. While they sat there, he kept checking with them again and again to see if they had changed their minds about buying a candy bar. It was amazing how many people changed their minds if he checked enough times.

Sunday afternoon was Danny's last chance. He stood outside a bookstore telling people that some of the best reading was on candy bar wrappers. He sold two candy bars, which gave him a total of seventy-nine. He wanted to break the magic eighty barrier, but after a while people started yelling at him when he mentioned the subject of candy bars.

The store closed at five o'clock, and Danny headed home. On his way, he passed a toy store that was also closed. Sitting on the front steps was someone with a familiar face. It was the boy who lived in the house with three children and Maximum Clyde music. Danny was getting another chance to break the magic eighty barrier.

"Hello," Danny said.

"Go away," said the boy. Then he looked up at Danny. "I've seen you before. You were looking through my window."

The boy was not smiling. But Danny was. Danny was smiling as hard as he could, trying to think of something to say.

Finally he said, "I was not looking through your window."

The boy grabbed Danny's arm and squeezed. Danny said, "I was *listening* through your window."

"What do you mean by that?" asked the boy. He squeezed harder, like Danny's arm was a giant tube of toothpaste. Something came out, but it was not toothpaste. It was two words.

"Maximum Clyde," gulped Danny.

As Danny Dorfman says the magic words a door opens up in the huge, rocky cliff. It slides back to show a city that is ten times as big as Chicago. All the buildings are shaped like guitars. The people are dressed up like they are in a rock band. When they pass somebody on the street, they make a secret sign and say, "Maximum Clyde." The other person answers, "Maximum Clyde."

MAXIMUM CLYDE

"Maximum Clyde," Danny says at an ice cream store. The owner gives him a hot-fudge sundae.

"Maximum Clyde," Danny says to a police officer. The officer presents him with a special award for bravery.

A truck is coming straight toward Danny. He murmurs, "Maximum Clyde," and it stops one inch from Danny's nose.

It is a whole Maximum Clyde city. You can get whatever you want by saying those magic words.

The boy let go of Danny's arm and said, "Do you like Maximum Clyde?"

"That's why I came to this fabulous city," Danny answered.

"What fabulous city?" asked the boy.

"Never mind," said Danny.

Danny tried to think of a way to start talking about candy bars casually. But the boy, whose name was Garth, wanted to talk about Maximum Clyde. Garth said he liked Maximum Clyde's newest smash hit, "Totally." It was called that because *totally* was the only word in the song.

"Maybe you could come to my house sometime and listen to Maximum Clyde tapes," Garth said.

Danny remembered the last time he had gone to Garth's house. "When I was there before," he asked, "why didn't you answer the door?"

Garth looked away. He seemed angry again. Then he just seemed tired. "I am not supposed to answer the door when I babysit," he said.

Danny was surprised that a boy who

squeezed your arm would also babysit. He found out that Garth's mother and father both worked. Garth went to a different school from Danny, and every day when school was over, Garth had to take care of his sister and two brothers. He had to stay home almost all the time. The only reason he had been allowed to leave today was to buy a present for his little sister. Tomorrow was her birthday.

"But I got here too late," said Garth. "The stores are all closed."

Danny thought of what it must be like to spend your whole life babysitting. He wondered how Garth must feel not to have a present for his little sister. Then Danny remembered what was in the box at his side, and he smiled.

"I might be able to help you," he said.

Chapter Seven

"Thank you for coming to our special assembly," said Mr. McBee, the school principal. "It is special because we will find out who won the contest for selling candy bars. It is also special because we are going to see some slides."

The students groaned. It was another one of Mr. McBee's famous slide shows. No matter what was happening at

Saddler Street School, Mr. McBee had slides of it. He would show the slides to anybody who would watch. If no one would watch, he would call an assembly and make people watch.

It was Monday, and Danny was in the school auditorium. He looked behind him and saw the members of the great Danny Dorfman Band sitting with their classes. Rodney was leaning back, looking cool. Anna had an armlock on the boy next to her. Winifred was just being Winifred, which meant telling everybody in the area what to do.

The lights went down, and Mr. McBee started showing his slides. They were pictures of things the school was going to buy with money from the candy bar sale. The first slide showed a drawing of a new sign in front of the school. It said PTA MEETING! TONIGHT! WELCOME, PARENTS! Danny could tell Mr. McBee had drawn the picture because he always put exclamation marks after everything.

While Mr. McBee talked, somebody poked Danny's shoulder. He turned around and saw little sparkles of light in the dark area behind him. The sparkles were in the shape of a mouth. It was Mimi Spinoli's Jaws of Death, reflecting Mr. McBee's slides.

"Too bad, Danny Dorfman," she whispered. "You are going to lose the contest. Because I am going to win."

Danny wanted to say something back to her, but he couldn't think of anything. He just stared at the sparkles.

He wished Anna were sitting next to him so she could put an armlock on Mimi Spinoli.

Then Danny had a terrible thought. What if the cheating Spinoli twins really did win the contest? What if they and two of their sweet little friends went to see Maximum Clyde, and the great Danny Dorfman Band had to stay home? It was one of the worst things Danny had thought about in his whole life.

Mr. McBee's slides kept going on and on. He showed a flagpole with a big American flag. He showed a new piano for the band room. Then he ran out of things the school would buy, and he started showing slides on dental health. Soon Danny knew all about gum disease.

Finally Mr. McBee turned the lights back on. "And now," he said, "we will find out who won our big candy bar contest!"

The people who were not asleep cheered. Danny got a tingly feeling in his stomach. In just a few minutes, he would know whether he and his band would be going to see Maximum Clyde.

"First of all," said Mr. McBee, "raise your hand if you sold more than ten candy bars."

Danny looked around the auditorium. There were so many hands that it looked like a jungle of hands.

"Excellent!" said Mr. McBee. "Now, raise your hand if you sold more than twenty candy bars."

The jungle got a little smaller.

"More than thirty candy bars," he said.

The jungle got a lot smaller.

"More than forty."

The jungle didn't look like a jungle anymore. It just looked like hands.

"Everyone whose hand is raised, please come to the front of the auditorium and stand next to me," said Mr. McBee.

Fifteen people walked up to the front. Four of them were the great Danny Dorfman Band. Another one was Mimi Spinoli. She stood right next to Danny. Her Jaws of Death were smiling in the front, but on the side they were whispering, "You will lose, Danny Dorfman."

"Let's give these kids a big round of

applause," Mr. McBee said. Everybody clapped. Mimi did a little curtsy, like she was a ballerina of some kind. It made Danny sick just to watch it.

"Who will the winner be?" asked Mr. McBee. "Who will get four tickets to the Maximum Clyde concert? Now we will find out."

He turned to the fifteen people. "If you sold fewer than fifty candy bars, please sit down."

Eight of the people sat down, including Winifred and Anna.

"Fewer than sixty candy bars," he said.

Rodney went to his seat, along with two other people. That left Danny, Mimi, Gary Higgenbottom, and Virgil Gauze.

"Fewer than seventy."

Gary and Virgil sat down. It was just Danny and Mimi. Danny's stomach felt more tingly than ever.

"Fewer than eighty," said Mr. McBee.

Danny waited for Mimi to sit down. But she never moved. Mimi Spinoli had broken the magic eighty barrier!

"How many candy bars did you sell?" Mr. McBee asked Mimi and Danny.

"Eighty," said Mimi.

"Eighty-one!" yelled Danny.

He jumped up and down all around the front of the auditorium. He was going to the Maximum Clyde concert!

Partly it was because of Danny, who had worked hard. Partly it was because of the Spinoli twins, who had not

worked hard enough. But mostly it was because of Garth's little sister, who loved chocolate so much that Garth had bought her two candy bars instead of just one.

Chapter Eight

The next day, the Danny Dorfman Band was going to have a special practice. In honor of Danny's great victory they would play Maximum Clyde music. They would perform "Toe Jam," "I Love Cockroaches," and many other awesome favorites. But when Anna, Rodney, and Winifred went into the garage after school, there was a problem.

"My drums!" said Anna.

"My bass!" said Rodney.

"My piano thing!" said Winifred.

The instruments were gone. Besides the drums, bass, and piano thing, Danny's guitar was missing. The garage was so empty there was room for a car. It just didn't seem right.

"What are we going to do?" asked Anna.

"We could try humming the songs," Winifred suggested, but the others did not like that idea.

They went into the house looking for Danny. They found him in his room.

"How can you just sit there?" asked Anna. "The Danny Dorfman Band is ruined!" She told him about the missing instruments.

"No biggie," said Danny.

"If I sit on you, that will be a biggie," Anna said.

"Please follow me," Danny said. He walked out of the house and across the front yard. The band followed him to the Dorfmans' minivan, which was parked on the street. Danny opened the door.

"My drums!" said Anna.

"My bass!" said Rodney.

"My piano thing!" said Winifred.

"And my guitar," said Danny. "The Danny Dorfman Band is not ruined. It is just going on a trip."

They got into the minivan, and Mrs. Dorfman drove them down the street. Anna asked Danny, "Does this trip have anything to do with your great victory in the contest?"

"Sort of."

"Yo," said Rodney, "can I see the tickets you won?"

"I don't have them," he said.

Winifred asked, "Where are they?"

"I gave them away," said Danny.

The band members did not say anything. They just stared at Danny like he had suddenly turned purple and grown six or seven noses.

"Isn't that nice?" said his mother.

"No," said Winifred, "it is scary."

"I hope you are not mad," Danny said.

"Not about the concert," Anna told Danny. "But you worked very hard to win those tickets."

"Someone else worked harder," he said.

Danny told them about Garth, who had to stay home every day to watch his sister and brothers. Danny explained that Garth's parents worked, and Garth did not have much money to spend on things like concerts. Then Danny told them Garth had used that little bit of money to buy the birthday present of two candy bars that had broken the magic eighty barrier and won the contest.

"I like candy bars," Danny said, "but they are not much of a birthday present. A better present would be a live concert by the great Danny Dorfman Band. Plus four tickets to a Maximum Clyde concert."

"Cool," said Rodney.

The minivan parked in front of the small house that had weeds growing in the yard. Danny jumped out and knocked on the front door. This time somebody answered. It was Garth. His little sister was standing behind him. She peeked out and smiled.

Garth opened the garage, and the band set up their instruments inside. Garth and his sister and brothers gathered outside. When the band was ready, Danny held up his hand for silence.

"Thank you, ladies and gentlemen," he said. "This afternoon the great Danny Dorfman Band is going to play some Maximum Clyde songs. This special performance is in honor of Garth's little sister. It is also in honor of Garth, who is the number-two Maximum Clyde fan in the whole world."

Danny counted off, and the music began.

It is the first night of rock superstar Danny Dorfman's world tour. As he

starts to play, thousands of people cheer in some strange kind of foreign language. He cannot understand what they are saying, but it doesn't matter. He knows they worship him.

In the audience is Danny's old friend, the crown prince of Moravia. The prince's little sister is with him. The music is so awesome they cannot sit still. They are dancing around just like regular people.

After the concert, Danny is mobbed by his many Moravian fans. He and his band are invited to the palace for a feast with the prince. They are served all the finest foods Moravia has to offer.

"Do you want any more Coke and chips?" asked Garth.

Danny shook his head. He had a

smile on his face and was gazing off across the kitchen.

"Thank you for the concert," said Garth. "And thank you again for the tickets."

Danny murmured, "It is nothing, old friend."

"Will you snap out of it?" said Winifred.

Garth looked across the table at Anna. "Is he all right?"

Anna smiled. "He is just fine," she said.

Danny Dorfman's Dream Band

Win Danny's Guitar Contest

Official Rules

1. Entrants must be U.S. or Canadian residents between the ages of 7 and 12 as of January 1, 1992.

2. Mail all entries to: **Danny Dorfman Contest, Puffin Marketing Dept., Penguin USA, 375 Hudson Street, New York, NY 10014.** Entries must be received by December 31st, 1992. One per person, please.

3. Winner will be selected through a random drawing conducted on January 15, 1993 by an appointed judge. Winner will be notified by mail.

4. The guitar awarded may differ from guitar pictured on book covers. Prize is non-transferable.

5. Employees and their families of Penguin USA and its affiliates may not enter this contest. This offer is void where prohibited and subject to all federal, state and local laws.

6. For the name of the prize winner, send a self-addressed, stamped envelope to: Danny Dorfman Contest, Puffin Books Marketing Dept., Penguin USA, 375 Hudson Street, New York, NY 10014.